© 1995 Twin Books Ltd

Produced by
TWIN BOOKS
Kimbolton House
117a Fulham Road
London SW3 6RL

Directed by CND – Muriel Nathan-Deiller
Illustrated by Van Gool-Lefèvre-Loiseaux

ISBN: 1 85469 781 1

Printed in China

Jungle Book

Van Gool

TWIN BOOKS

One hot summer's evening, Shere Khan, the fierce tiger, was prowling through the jungle. Suddenly a strange sound echoed through the trees – a baby crying! At once the tiger began to follow the sound. He came into a clearing and saw a tiny human baby crawling at the edge of the river. He was just about to attack when two wolves leaped out of the bushes. "Leave the child alone, Shere Khan!" they growled.

Shere Khan was in no mood for a fight, and he slunk back into the jungle. "One day the child will be mine," he roared, "Then I will kill him!" "We must protect this man-child," said Mother Wolf, licking the baby as if he were one of her cubs. Father Wolf agreed. "We must ask Akela and the pack for their help," he decided.

That night when the wolf pack met at Council Rock, Father Wolf told them about the man-cub. "We have called him Mowgli," he said. "Do you agree that we should protect him from Shere Khan?" The wolves muttered among themselves. Just then a voice came from the other side of the meeting place. "I will help bring up the child," said Baloo the Bear.

"Baloo and I will teach Mowgli the Law of the Jungle," called Bagheera, the sleek, black panther. Finally the wolves agreed that the human child should stay with them. "Mowgli is now one of the pack," declared Akela, the pack leader.

As the years passed, Mowgli grew up strong and brave. Baloo and Bagheera taught him how to hunt and look after himself. They introduced him to all the creatures in the jungle, and taught Mowgli their languages. Mowgli felt at home in the jungle, and all the animals accepted him as one of their own. All except one.

For Shere Khan had returned to the jungle, and when he heard that Mowgli was alive and well, he was very angry. "The man-cub has been lucky, but I will have my revenge!" he roared. Baloo and Bagheera warned Mowgli to be careful. "Shere Khan will kill you if he can," they told him. But Mowgli just laughed. "I'm not afraid of him," he replied. "I can take care of myself."

One afternoon while Baloo and Bagheera dozed in the sun, the monkeys came to visit Mowgli. Most of the animals in the jungle despised the monkeys, because all they did was play games and silly tricks. However, Mowgli thought they were great fun. "Come with us, Mowgli," they called. "We've got something to show you." Mowgli climbed up into the trees and followed them.

When Baloo and Bagheera awoke, there was no sign of Mowgli. "Where can the boy be?" asked Baloo worriedly. They looked for him everywhere, but found no trace of him. Suddenly Kaa the snake slithered up to them. "I hear you are looking for Mowgli," he hissed. "I saw him playing with the monkeys. I think they have taken him to their hideout. Come, I will take you there."

Although Mowgli had enjoyed playing with the monkeys, he soon became tired, and wanted to leave. But they would not let him go. "You belong to us now!" they hooted, grabbing hold of his arms and legs. "Let go of me!" cried Mowgli, struggling to get free. The monkeys just held on even tighter.

23

The monkeys' hideout was an old ruined village, and Kaa showed Baloo and Bagheera how to creep inside. With a terrifying roar the panther and the bear leaped into the middle of the monkeys. The monkeys had a terrible shock, but they wanted to keep Mowgli, and fought ferociously. Baloo and Bagheera fought bravely, but there were just too many monkeys.

Forced into a deep pool by the monkeys, Baloo and Bagheera thought they were surely beaten. Just then Kaa slithered into the fight. At the sight of the giant snake the monkeys began to howl in terror, and ran away. Mowgli was very glad to see his friends, and very sorry that he had caused them so much trouble. "Thank you for saving me," he said. "I won't play with the monkeys again!"

A few evenings later the wolves were gathered at Council Rock when Shere Khan stalked into their meeting. "Why do you let that man-child stay with you?" he asked. "If I were you I'd drive him back to the village where he belongs." Some of the wolves admired the tiger, and they called out in agreement. "After all, he is not a wolf," they cried. Mowgli leaped on to the highest rock. "If that is what you want I shall leave," he said sadly. "But do not think you have won, Shere Khan."

Mowgli wanted to teach the tiger a lesson, so he ran through the jungle to the man-village. He stole a pot of hot coals from outside one of the huts, and hurried back to Council Rock. Just before he reached the meeting place he stopped and lit a torch from the coals.

31

When Mowgli entered the clearing carrying the flaming torch, the tiger shrank back in fear. Mowgli had remembered one of Bagheera's lessons – that all animals were afraid of fire, even the terrible tiger. Mowgli waved the torch in front of Shere Khan's nose and the tiger ran howling back into the trees. "There is your hero now!" cried Mowgli, scornfully.

Later that night Mowgli sat talking with his friend, Grey Brother. "Shere Khan will be back," he said. "And he wants to kill me more than ever now. If I stay here I will only be a danger to you all. Perhaps he is right and I don't belong in the jungle." Sadly he decided to go to the man village.

At first the villagers were suspicious of Mowgli because he had come out of the jungle. They thought he was strange because he did not speak their language, and slept under the stars every night. But soon they trusted him, and set him to work tending their buffalo. One evening Grey Brother and Father Wolf came to visit Mowgli. "Shere Khan is back," said the wolf. "He is sleeping in a cornfield nearby."

Mowgli gathered his herd and led them to the tiger's lair. As soon as the buffalo smelt the tiger they panicked and stampeded. Before Shere Khan had a chance to escape, the frightened animals had trampled him under their hooves.

Mowgli took the tiger's skin back to the village. But the villagers threw stones and sticks at him. Many of the bravest men had tried to kill the tiger and failed. They did not believe that a boy could have beaten the savage animal, and thought he was a sorcerer. "Go away!" they cried, "Children don't kill tigers – you're not human!"

Driven away by man, Mowgli returned to the jungle. He hung the tiger skin over a tree, and waited while Bagheera called the wolves to Council Rock. When they saw that Mowgli had killed the great tiger, the wolves who had wanted him to leave were very ashamed. "Please stay with us, Mowgli," they begged. "You do belong in the jungle. You are one of us!"

Mowgli was glad they wanted him to stay, for he knew that he could never go back to the man-village again. Once again he hunted with the young wolves and sat in the sun with his friends, Baloo and Bagheera. He was happy to be back in the jungle where he belonged.